Three Together

igloo

Published in 2008
by Igloo Books Ltd
Cottage Farm,
Sywell,
NN6 0BJ
www.igloo-books.com

10 9 8 7 6 5 4 3 2 1

ISBN: 978 1 84561 930 5

Cover design by Insight Design
Cover illustrated by © Rachel Ellen Designs Ltd
Interior illustrations by Liz and Kate Pope

Printed and manufactured in China

The Mystery of the Dark House

by Carol Lawrence

igloo

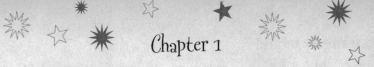

Chapter 1

The Secret of the Garden

"Here, boy! Jasper, come here!" Giving up, Poppy ran to Jasper, instead, and gave him a hug.

It was the school holidays, and nine-year old Poppy, who had black hair and sparkling green eyes, was playing in the back garden with her best friend, KC. Poppy's seven-and-a-half year old brother, Sam, who was often to be found where the girls were, was playing with them. The three friends were always at each other's houses.

Jasper was running everywhere. He'd already upset KC's cat, Millie, by trying to play with her. Now Millie was safely on the window sill, keeping a close eye on Jasper to make sure he didn't come too close. Jasper was leaping around the garden, his tongue lolling out and his long ears flying backwards.

"Come to me, Jasper!" KC called. KC didn't like big, loud dogs, but Jasper was so friendly that no one could resist him, even if he was acting a little strangely today!

Suddenly, Jasper lifted his nose. He sniffed, and gave a puzzled "Woof!" Then he dived right into the thick hedge at the edge of the garden.

"Where did he go?" asked Sam.

Sam loved playing on computers better than anything, but he wasn't going to let Poppy and KC have all the fun with Jasper.

"Jasper! Come back!" called Poppy. But there was no sound from the hedge.

Poppy stuck her head into the hedge.

"Jasper?"

All she could see was leaves. She pushed through

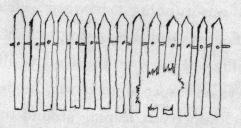

the hedge until she could make out the fence behind it. The bottom of the fence was rotten, and there was a large gap in it. Looking through, Poppy could see into the garden next door. Leaves scattered the grass, which was rough and overgrown. Jasper frolicked in the leaves, grinning at Poppy.

"Bad Jasper!" Poppy called. "Come back here!" But Jasper just jumped and barked at her, as if to say, "Come on in!"

Poppy crawled back out. "We have to go and get him."

"No way, Poppy!" said KC. "I'm not going in there! That's the garden of the Dark House!"

The house next door to Poppy's parent's house had been empty for months. Without really thinking about it, Poppy, KC and Sam had started calling it the Dark House. It looked like Poppy and Sam's house on the outside, but that's where the similarity stopped. The Dark House looked as though it would be cold and dusty, with draughty rooms and dark corners, not warm and cosy like Poppy and Sam's home.

Jasper barked over the fence.

"We still have to get him back," Poppy said. "I'm going in."

KC and Sam looked at each other. "So am I," they said at the same time, which made them laugh.

Poppy crawled into the hedge, and through the

hole in the fence. It was only just big enough for her to get through. She stood up and looked around.

The air seemed colder over here. The garden was dense and overgrown. The trees at the back seemed to stoop over to reach Poppy's head. Above the garden, the Dark House itself stood cold and blank.

KC and Sam struggled through the hole. "Wow," said Sam. "Spooky."

Even KC was excited. "We should look around. Before we go back, I mean."

Poppy grabbed Jasper's collar and stroked him. "It can't hurt to explore a little," she said.

The garden was full of surprises. In one corner, a little statue of a winged child seemed to watch them with wide stone eyes. They found a path that led to a pond, all covered in green so it looked almost like part of the grass. Some bright red flowers peeped out of a tangled flower bed. Before they realised it, they had explored the whole garden, and the daylight was starting to fade. They ran back into the middle of the lawn, and looked up at the Dark House.

"That place is really creepy," said KC.

"I bet it's all dusty and full of spiders' webs," Sam said.

KC shivered. "Let's go back," she said.

They turned to go, when Poppy saw something out of the corner of her eye. She looked up at the Dark House, all the way up to the attic. In the tiny window that faced Poppy's house, Poppy saw a strange, blue light glowing. She stopped KC and Sam. "Look up there! Do you see it too?"

"Someone's in the house," said Sam. "Let's get out of here!"

Grabbing Jasper, they ran back to the hedge. KC and Sam slid under the fence. Poppy pushed Jasper through the hole, and scrambled through. She looked up anxiously at the blue light in the attic. Had anybody seen them? As she watched, the light faded . . . and went out.

Chapter 2

A Boy Called Nicholas

"What do you think it was?" asked KC as they went inside. "Did someone move in?"

Poppy's mum and dad were inside. "Sam," said Poppy's mum, "how did you get so much dirt on your jeans?"

Poppy asked who lived in the Dark House.

"A man lived there, but he moved out. It's empty right now," said Poppy's dad, "but I think he still owns it."

The friends looked at each other. Empty houses don't have lights on.

"If the house is empty, can we go inside?" asked Poppy.

Her parents looked at her and frowned. "Poppy, you know that would be wrong," said her dad.

"Not to mention dangerous," said Poppy's mum.

"If it's empty, how can it be dangerous?" Poppy wanted to know.

"Because," said her mum, and went back to helping Poppy's dad with the cooking. Poppy rolled her eyes. Why was it that grown-ups could be so exasperating sometimes?

The friends were interested. They went out the front door to see if there was anything strange-looking about the Dark House from the front. But when they saw it next to Poppy's house, sitting quietly on the street, it looked perfectly ordinary. KC looked up at it suspiciously. "You'd never know it was so weird from the front. That's unfair."

Poppy giggled. "It should have towers, and bats coming out of it!"

The three friends looked up at the Dark House. Heavy curtains covered the windows, and they couldn't see any light shining through. A half-open gate led to an alley at the side of the house. "If we went down that alley," thought Poppy, "we'd come out in that spooky back garden again."

"Poppy!" a voice called out from down the street. "Is that you?"

They turned to see a boy walking towards them. He was scruffy and thin, with a mop of untidy brown hair that almost hid his eyes.

"Nicholas!" Poppy said. Nicholas was in Poppy's class at school. He wasn't very loud, and he wasn't top of the class, and he wasn't best at sports. He didn't talk a lot, but when he did say something, it was interesting.

"How's Edgar?" asked KC.

Nicholas pulled out a matchbox and opened it a tiny bit. "He's great, thanks," he said.

"Who's Edgar?" asked Sam.

"My pet spider," said Nicholas. "He goes with me everywhere, in his own little house. At night, I let him out, but he always comes back in the morning."

Sam backed away a little. He wasn't sure he wanted to see a spider. "Don't worry, Sam," said Nicholas. "Look!" He opened the matchbox a little bit more, and Sam peeked in. Edgar was tiny; just a small dot with legs, scurrying around in the matchbox.

"Nicholas loves animals," Poppy explained. "He's always got some kind of pet." Nicholas nodded.

"Anyway, what's happening?" asked KC. "I didn't know you lived around here, Nicholas."

"I don't," said Nicholas, looking nervous, suddenly. "I'm just walking around."

Poppy noticed that Nicholas had a pair of binoculars around his neck. He was also carrying some red flowers. Poppy thought the flowers looked familiar.

"Where are you going?" asked KC.

"You tell me what 'KC' stands for, KC, and I'll tell you," said Nicholas, grinning.

"As if," smiled KC. "That's my biggest secret! Nobody knows. Not even Poppy. Mum says it adds to my feminine mystique."

"Then I'll keep my walks secret, too," said Nicholas. "Maybe I'll tell you, one of these days."

Whatever it was, Nicholas looked excited. "Anyhow, I've got to be getting home now." He nodded goodbye and then walked off down the road.

Poppy knew that meetings with Nicholas were always a little odd like that. It was why she liked him.

"We forgot to tell him about the Dark House," said Sam. "I bet he would have liked to hear about it. Maybe we could have used his binoculars to look inside!"

It was starting to get really dark, so Poppy, KC and Sam went back inside Poppy and Sam's house. They climbed the stairs to Poppy's room, and took out some games to play. But none of Poppy's games seemed as exciting as the Dark House and its strange light.

"What should we do?" Sam wondered. "It's a mystery."

"You're right," said Poppy. "And you know what we do with mysteries. We solve them! Let's go up to the attic room. We can probably see the Dark House from there."

The attic room was right at the top of the house. Poppy loved this little room. The roof sloped

in over the side and made it look different, and exciting. It had one little window, with a broad window sill. They climbed onto the sill and looked out. They could see the attic window of the Dark House, right opposite them. It was just a square black hole. There was no sign of any blue light at all. They squinted and tried to look through the window, but they couldn't see anything at all. The window was too tiny, and the inside of the attic was just too dark.

Sam sighed. "It's useless," he said. "There's nothing there."

"We all saw it, Sam," said KC. "It was real." Sam and KC climbed down from the sill.

Poppy kept looking, as if she could light up the attic of the Dark House with her eyes.

She caught a sudden movement, but it wasn't from the attic. In the window right below the attic, she saw a figure dash past. It moved too quickly through the gloom of the house to see what it looked like.

Poppy called to Sam and KC, who came running back. "Quick, quick!" said Poppy, straining her eyes to see in the dark. "Down there!" By the time KC and Sam had climbed onto the sill again, there was nothing to see.

Poppy opened the window. "Stay still," said Poppy. "I can hear something." They listened. Poppy was right! There was the sound of a door opening outside, just below them.

Poppy, KC and Sam raced downstairs, almost tripping in their hurry, right to the kitchen window. The fence was too high to see over it, into the alley, but it seemed to them that it moved, as if someone were on the other side. "They're leaving!" said Poppy. "Quick, the front door!"

They dashed to the front door and opened it, but there was no one in sight. The only thing moving was a whoosh of leaves that had been stirred up. Whoever it was, they must have dashed around the corner and out of sight.

The friends looked at each other. "I knew it!" said Poppy.

KC stayed as long as she could at Poppy's house, so they could talk about what they'd seen.

"Was it a girl?" asked Sam.

"No way," said Poppy. "It was a definitely a boy. I think!"

"I bet it was a grown up," said KC.

"But how did they get away so quickly?" asked Poppy. "We ran down right after them, and they were already gone!"

"Whatever," said Sam. "It's probably the man who owns the house. You know, the one Dad told us about."

Poppy had her thinking face on. "I don't get it," she said. "If it was the person who lives in the house, then why didn't he switch on the lights?"

"KC!" Poppy's dad called up the stairs. "It's getting late. I'll take you home in the car."

"Anyway," said Poppy as she said goodbye to KC, "there really is a mystery in the Dark House. And we're going to solve it!"

Chapter 3

The Strange Man

The next morning, KC came over early. Poppy and Sam were waiting for her in the kitchen. Poppy had doodled a picture of the Dark House and coloured in the strange glow at the top.

"I've been thinking," Poppy said. "We need to find out about who lived in the house before."

"How do we do that?" asked Sam. "I can check on the internet."

Poppy shook her head. "No," she said. "It's time to ask some questions!"

"But who are we going to speak to?" asked KC, drawing some flowers onto the garden of Poppy's house.

"It needs to be someone who knows everything about the street. Someone who's been here for years. Someone who will talk to us about everything they know," said Poppy thoughtfully.

Sam frowned "Oh no. You don't mean . . ."

"Oh, yes, I do," said Poppy, getting up. "Mrs.

Linder!"

Poppy pressed the doorbell of Mrs. Linder's house. It was right opposite theirs. Sam looked annoyed.

"Why don't you like Mrs. Linder?" KC asked.

"You'll see," said Sam.

Mrs. Linder opened the door with a shriek of delight. "Hello, hello!" she said. She was a small woman with bright eyes that darted around as she talked. She grabbed Sam and tousled his hair. "Little Sam-Sam!" she said, holding him tightly. "I can't believe how big you are! Why, it seems just a minute ago that you were no bigger than my shoe!" She covered his face with kisses. Sam scrunched up his face and tried to pretend he wasn't there. KC tried not to laugh.

"Hello, Mrs. Linder," said Poppy, "We were wondering, who used to live in the house next door to ours?"

Mrs. Linder frowned. "Come inside," she said.

Mrs. Linder brought out some dry-looking biscuits. Sam had to sit next to her. He didn't say anything, but Poppy and KC could tell by the look on his face he would rather be somewhere else.

"That house," said Mrs. Linder. "Goodness me. I was glad when Mr. Faltermeyer left."

"Is that the name of the man who lived in the house?" Poppy asked.

"That's right," said Mrs. Linder. "He was a strange man. He was mean, and bad-tempered."

KC nudged Poppy to ask some more. "Why?" Poppy asked. "What did he do?"

"He always argued! He never listened to my advice, and he always frowned."

"We thought we saw someone in his house last night," said KC, taking another biscuit. "I mean, we really, definitely, did see someone. Could Mr. Faltermeyer be back?"

Mrs. Linder thought for a second. "I would have known," she said. "There's not much I don't see around here. No, I don't think he's back. But you can never be sure with Mr. Faltermeyer. Maybe he sneaked back in."

"But we didn't see anyone outside yesterday," said Poppy. "The only person we saw was Nicholas."

"Oh, yes?" Mrs. Linder perked up. "And who is Nicholas?"

They told her. "Hmm," said Mrs. Linder. "He sounds like a strange child."

"I've just remembered something," said Poppy. "Nicholas was carrying some red flowers. They looked like the same kind of flowers we saw in the garden of the Dark House. You can see them over the fence," added Poppy quickly. She didn't want Mrs. Linder to know they'd been in the garden of the Dark House!

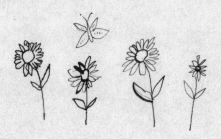

Mrs. Linder nodded. "That proves it. It'll be this Nicholas. Fooling around in someone else's house!"

The friends looked at each other and shook their heads. It seemed rude to disagree with Mrs. Linder, but talking about Nicholas that way just didn't seem right. "Um, I guess it could have been him,"

Poppy said eventually.

Mrs. Linder nodded. "Oh, yes. Well, don't worry. I'll keep an eye out for him. And if I see him sneaking around again, there'll be trouble!"

Chapter 4

The Spooky Voice

The three friends said goodbye to Mrs. Linder. Sam just managed to avoid getting hugged again.

They went back into Poppy's house, and straight out to the back garden, making sure that Jasper was safely inside the house. They looked over the fence at the Dark House, but couldn't see anything through the dusty windows.

KC remembered what Mrs. Linder had said about Nicholas. "It can't be Nicholas we saw in the Dark House," she said. "Can it?"

Poppy shook her head. "No way. He may like going around on his own, and he may be a little different, but he's not the kind of person who would go into someone else's house. He did say he had a secret, though."

"I think it's that man," said Sam, "Mr. Faltermeyer. I think he's come back."

"We should go back through the hole in the fence and investigate," said Poppy. "We need to find some clues! We can't let Mrs. Linder think it was Nicholas."

"I don't know, Poppy," said KC, looking doubtful. "What if we get seen? And I don't like that garden. It's kind of spooky."

"That's okay, KC," said Poppy. "You can stay here if you want."

"No way!" said KC. "If you're going, I'm coming with you! You might need my help!"

So Poppy, KC and Sam squeezed themselves through the gap into the garden of the Dark House once more.

"This time," said Poppy, "we should look for clues. Maybe the person in the house has been out here, and left something behind."

Sam looked around at the tall grass. "I don't think anyone has been out here for a long time."

Still, the friends began to look around carefully this time. KC even got up the courage to examine the little winged statue, but it didn't seem to hold any clues.

Poppy looked down. The thick, high grass was still wet with dew. Wherever the friends went, they left big trails of pale, flattened grass, gleaming in the pale morning sun.

"I wonder," Poppy said, and went over to one of the big trees near the bottom of the garden. She saw a low branch and climbed up. There was another, bigger branch just above that one, and Poppy pulled herself up on to it. From here, she could see over the whole garden. The paths the friends had left were pale green streaks, but there was another path, one that wasn't so clear.

She climbed down and found KC and Sam. "Did you two go over to the house yesterday?" she asked.

They shook their heads. "We didn't go anywhere near it - and neither did Jasper," said KC. "He was sticking his nose into those overgrown flowerbeds most of the time, remember?"

"That's weird," said Poppy. "Because there's a

trail of flat grass. It goes all the way to the back door of the Dark House!"

The friends followed the path cautiously as it trailed back to the house. The grass wasn't as fresh or flattened as their recent trails.

"This must have happened yesterday," guessed Poppy, "before we came out here."

She looked at the house as they got closer.

At the back door, the friends peered into the large window next to it.

There was no light or movement coming from inside the house but, in the sunlight, they could see through the window. The kitchen was dusty. Everything looked faded and neglected and sad. Spiders' webs hung from work surfaces, and a couple of dead flies lay on the windowsill. "Doesn't look like anyone's been in there, either," said Sam.

"But someone has," said Poppy. "See down there?"

She pointed to another trail through the grass from the door. This one led down the side of the house, to the alley that ran down to the front. It was filled with all sorts of junk.

"Whoever we saw last night came around this way," said Poppy. "I bet that door to the front isn't locked!"

But nobody wanted to go into the alley. It just seemed wrong; almost like going into the house itself.

Poppy looked back at the kitchen door and made a decision. She walked over to it and, very gently, turned the handle.

The door opened without a sound. She quickly closed it again, her fingers trembling.

"Poppy!" said KC.

"It's okay," said Poppy, stepping away from the door. "I wasn't going to go in. I just wanted to see."

"Why would it be unlocked?" asked Sam.

"Mum and Dad told us we weren't allowed inside." Poppy was glad that her parents had told her not to go inside, because she wasn't sure she wanted to enter the Dark House right now, anyway. "We should go."

It was then that they heard the voice from the back of the garden.

"Whooo are yoooou?" it called. "Whoooo are yoooou?"

Poppy, KC and Sam jumped. They looked around, but there was nobody there.

"Whooo are yoooou?" the voice called again.

They looked at each other. Poppy could see that KC was frightened.

"Don't worry," she said, squeezing KC's hand. "Let's go find out who it is."

KC looked at Poppy, her eyes shining. "How can you be so brave all the time, Poppy?"

Poppy stepped towards the trees. She looked braver than she felt. Her heart was thumping, but something told her that the voice wasn't as scary as it sounded. Poppy passed the winged child statue. She tried not to stare at it. When the voice came again, she was quite relieved to find it was coming from beyond the statue, not actually from it!

"Who are you?" Poppy called back. "And where are you?"

The voice giggled. Not a ghostly giggle or a spooky laugh. A kind of snorting, silly giggle. The kind someone makes when they're trying not to laugh, and it comes out of their nose instead. Poppy rushed towards the trees on the far side of the garden, and pushed a branch out of the way.

Chapter 5

The Big Battle

"Whooo are yooooou?" said the person behind the branch, and then burst out laughing.

It was Jess, the girl who lived on the other side of the Dark House.

Poppy glared at her. "We weren't scared."

Jess looked at her and giggled again. "You weren't - but I bet KC and that brother of yours were!"

Jess was Poppy's age, but she always seemed older. She loved to play jokes on people, and she was always climbing trees, riding her bike and shouting.

"What are you doing?" Jess asked. "You shouldn't be in there."

"We're looking for clues," said Poppy, and told her about the mysterious light in the Dark House. "Did you ever see Mr. Faltermeyer, when he lived here?"

"Wow," said Jess, "That sounds awesome. A real mystery. Come over and I'll tell you what I know about Mr. Faltermeyer!"

Poppy, KC and Sam went back through the hole in the fence. They ran out the front door of Poppy's house, past the Dark House, to Jess's house. She let them in, and they went upstairs to her room.

Sam was very excited. "Do you still have SuperRobots?"

Jess snorted. "Huh! That old videogame! I gave that to a friend ages ago. I only play MegaRobots now!"

Sam's eyes widened. "You've got to let me play!"

Jess' room had a big TV and three games consoles. Her science experiments were scattered around. They were mostly things that had been burnt, or exploded, or thrown onto walls. But it wasn't the TV or the experiments that the friends saw first.

It was the huge, black telescope in the middle of the room.

"I got it for my birthday," said Jess, proudly. "It can magnify things up to 675 times!" Jess went up to it and stroked it lovingly. "I can see for miles with this!"

Poppy and KC looked at each other. They were both thinking the same thing. The telescope would be perfect for looking into the Dark House!

KC nudged Poppy. "We could see into the attic with that," she said.

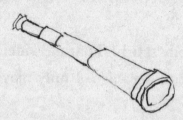

Jess looked at them. "What are you talking about?"

"Nothing," said Poppy. "So, did you ever see Mr. Faltermeyer?"

"No," said Jess. "My dad said that Mr. Faltermeyer was a strange man, though. He always stayed inside and never said hello to anyone. When he was in, you'd never even know he was there."

"Why not?" asked Poppy, excitedly.

"Because," said Jess, "he used to spend most of the time in the garden, even when it was dark. And there was only ever one light on in one room.

Why do you think it's called the Dark House?"

"I thought that was just our name for it," said Poppy.

"There are strange secrets there," said Jess. "What if the person you saw was Mr. Faltermeyer? What if he's been hiding inside all this time?"

"Why would he do that?" asked KC.

"I don't know," said Jess, switching on the TV and games console. "Like, what if he was building a maze inside the house, to trap anyone who went inside? Or, what if he locked himself in, ages ago, and he's just been eating tins of food and wandering around in the dark, trying to find the key? Or what if he's. . ."

"Those are all too silly," said Poppy. "I'm sure there's a good reason for the person in the house."

But Poppy didn't believe it. It seemed like anything could be happening inside the Dark House. And everyone seemed to have a different idea of what that was.

Just then, Sam saw two bright yellow devices with antennae, and picked one up. "Are those walkie-talkies?" he asked.

"Yes," said Jess, taking it from him. "Don't play around with them!"

Jess started playing MegaRobots. She turned the sound up until the friends could hardly hear themselves over the laser blasts and explosions. Jess was exterminating every enemy on the screen, and it didn't look like she was even trying.

"JESS!" shouted Poppy. "WE CAN FIND OUT . . ."

Jess turned the sound off suddenly, and Poppy was left shouting, "WHO'S IN THE HOUSE!"

Jess paused the game. She looked curious, even though she was trying not to. "How?"

Poppy explained. "We can take your telescope over to our house, and look into the attic of the Dark House!"

Jess started laughing. Poppy was starting to get annoyed at that laugh. Jess never seemed to include you in the joke. She liked laughing at you, not with you.

"As if!" Jess chuckled. "I'm not going to let a couple of girls and a baby mess around with my telescope!"

"You're a girl, too!" KC pointed out, and Sam added, "I'm not a baby!"

Jess looked at Sam. She narrowed her eyes. "Oh, yeah?" she said. "Prove it."

"How?" said Sam, looking a little scared.

Jess pointed to the TV. "Beat me at MegaRobots!"

"Oh," Sam faltered, "You look pretty good . . ."

"Oh, fine," said Jess. "If you're going to be chicken."

That was too much for Sam. He sat down next to her and grabbed a controller. "Let's do it," he said, trying to sound grown up.

"Wait!" said Poppy, before they could start. Jess and Sam looked at her, surprised. "If Sam wins, then we can borrow the telescope. Deal?"

Jess looked worried for a second, and then snorted. "Fine. Because Sam won't win! And if I win, what do I get?"

Poppy thought for a second, but KC spoke first. "We'll . . . do your chores for a week."

"Hmmm." Jess said. "Let's see. You could clean my bike, fix the tree-house, go into the muddy patch to get the football I lost in it, do all my homework and clean up my room." Poppy and KC looked around them at the dirty walls and messy floor. It would take hours, days, a whole week just to clean up this room!

"Okay, then," Jess said, with a wicked glint in her eye. "It's a deal."

Poppy grabbed Sam from where he was sitting. "You have to win," she said. "It's our only hope of finding out who's in the Dark House."

"I know all about MegaRobots," said Sam, nervously. "I read all about it on the internet. I know all the special moves and the characters and all the different powers. But there's one thing I haven't done."

"What's that?" asked Poppy.

"Played it!" admitted Sam. "Not even once!"

"Don't worry!" KC said. "It's the sequel to SuperRobots, right? And nobody beats you at that."

Sam nodded. "I'm the best at SuperRobots."

Poppy sat him back down. "Go for it, Sam!"

"We believe in you!" KC said.

Sam flexed his fingers. He breathed deeply. He picked up the game pad.

"Three lives each," said Jess. "Last one standing, wins." She pressed Start, and they were off.

Jess and Sam played so fast that Poppy and KC could hardly tell what was going on. Jess knew just where to look for secret power-ups, but Sam fought back bravely. He lost his first life quickly, and Jess punched the air and whooped. "Easy!" she said. But she wasn't laughing when Sam became invincible for a few seconds and attacked furiously.

Before long, both Sam and Jess each had one life left. Jess wasn't looking so happy now. She kept looking at Sam and frowning. But Sam didn't notice. He kept his eyes glued to the screen, and dodged every one of Jess's attacks. Jess flew into the air and zoomed down to try and take Sam by surprise, but he rolled out of the way. Then she tried vanishing and appearing next to him, but Sam spotted her trick. He summoned a laser attack, and Jess tried to dodge it. But she was too slow. "VICTORY!" appeared on the screen. Sam had won!

Poppy and KC grabbed him and gave him a hug.

They expected to see Jess looking angry or upset. But she was looking at Sam with respect.

"Not bad," Jess said. "I guess you're not a baby after all!"

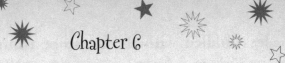

Chapter 6

Through the Telescope

Poppy, Jess and Sam carried the telescope up to Poppy's attic room. They had packed it up very carefully. Jess had insisted on coming, to make sure they used it properly. But Poppy thought that Jess wanted to find out more about the mystery, too.

The big telescope was soon set up. It looked out of the attic window. "We need something else," said Poppy, who'd been thinking hard. She ran downstairs and brought up a big torch. "This will help!"

Poppy shone the torch into the attic of the Dark House. Its beam only just reached through the window. It lightened up the gloom a little, but the friends still couldn't see anything clearly. The attic window was very small.

39

Jess fiddled with the telescope controls. "This should do the trick. Let me shine the torch in."

Poppy handed Jess the torch, and bent over to look through the eyepiece of the telescope. At first, she couldn't see a thing. Then she turned the focus knob that Jess had shown her. A black shape swam into view. It was a giant centipede!

Shocked, Poppy looked up, but there was only the attic window. She bent down again and zoomed out. The centipede was tiny, and it was sitting on the window sill of the attic. Poppy decided to keep her shock to herself. Poppy was the main mystery-solver, after all. She didn't want anyone thinking she was scared of a tiny insect.

Poppy moved the telescope a little, and looked back. She could see into the attic! Just by the window, it was light enough to see inside. But further back, it was dark. "Shine the torch in," said Poppy, and Jess aimed it at the inside of the attic.

At last, Poppy could see inside the Dark House. There were books and magazines piled up around an old, faded blue chair. To one side, there was a half-open trapdoor that she thought must lead down to the house below. It was very still. Somehow, the telescope made her feel as if she was inside the house, wandering around in the attic.

"Can you see any clues?" asked KC.

Poppy told them what she could see, and then let Sam and KC have a look. She took the torch from Jess, and pointed it through the window so that Jesse could look, too. "Nobody has been up there for ages," said Jess. "I reckon you three must be seeing things."

Poppy took another look through the telescope. "Someone has been up here recently." She zoomed in on a pile of magazines.

The amazing telescope was made to look at far-away galaxies in the sky. So it was easy to zoom in and read the titles of the magazines in the attic. "I can see a magazine with this month's date on it! Someone must have brought it up here not so long ago."

"See?" said Sam. "Poppy's awesome at finding things out! Anything else, Poppy?"

Poppy moved the telescope around slowly, looking at each area of the attic. "There's a notebook. Maybe it will give us a clue." She zoomed in a little more. Closer, closer . . . she could see words on a page of the notebook, which had been left lying against the chair. "I can read what it says! It says: very important: rowan, ash, lily, rose."

Poppy looked up from the telescope, but her friends looked just as puzzled as she was.

"Rowan and ash are trees," said Jess.

"We know that," said Sam. "Lily and rose are flowers."

"What's so important about writing down the names of plants in a book?" wondered Poppy. She put her eyes back to the telescope and searched for anything else that would help.

Suddenly there was a blur in front of the books. Poppy zoomed out . . . and saw that the trapdoor in the attic was opening!

"Jess!" she shouted. "Turn off the torch! Quick! Someone's coming up!"

Jess fumbled with the torch, as Poppy strained to see who it was who was coming up through the trapdoor. Jess switched it off, and the view from the telescope went dark again.

"Did you see anyone?" asked KC. Poppy shook her head.

"Did they see the torch light?" asked Jess.

"I don't know!" said Poppy. "Maybe . . ."

KC was already looking at the window below the attic. "I saw something! Whoever it is must have seen us trying to look in! They're running away again!"

Poppy was already running down the stairs before KC finished speaking. This time, she didn't go to the kitchen window. She flew down the stairs and went straight to the front door. She opened it and dashed outside. Surely, she would see something this time!

There was a clattering by the fence, and something zoomed off onto the street. It was a boy on a bike! Poppy ran out after him as he pedaled

furiously. There was no way she could keep up. A moment later, and the bike had disappeared around the corner. The street was empty, except for an older girl who was watching the bike go past.

KC, Sam and Jess came dashing out. "Did you see them?" asked KC.

"It's a 'him'," said Poppy. "I'm sure of it! He was on a bike. That's how he disappeared so quickly yesterday."

"Did you see his face?" asked Sam.

"No," said Poppy. "But I'm sure he wasn't a grown-up."

"You don't think," said KC, looking worried, "it could have been Nicholas, do you?"

Poppy stared down the road, as if she could see around the corner and far away to where the boy in the Dark House was. "I don't know. I don't think so, but who knows?"

The older girl strode up to them. She wore a denim jacket and had a streak of blonde in her dark hair. And she looked angry. "Whoever you are," she said, "You'd better stay away from this house!"

"What do you mean?" asked Poppy.

But the older girl was already walking off at speed. "It's too weird for you!" the strange girl called out. And then she turned the corner too, and was out of sight.

Poppy, KC and Sam offered to help Jess take her telescope back to her house. They were surprised when she said no.

"You guys keep it for a day or two," she said. "Just as long as you take really good care of it."

"Are you sure?" asked Poppy.

"Yes," Jess nodded. "Maybe we could look again tomorrow. In the attic, I mean. I bet that boy will come back!"

Meanwhile, KC had been writing down the names of the plants that Poppy had seen. "Rowan, Ash, Lily, Rose. Do you think that these are all plants in the garden of the Dark House, Poppy? And who was that girl?"

"I don't know," said Poppy. The clues didn't seem to make any sense. "We should check in the garden."

"Not now," said Sam, looking outside. "It's cold. And it'll be dark again soon. I don't want to go exploring that spooky garden in the dark!"

Even Jess didn't look like she wanted to do that.

"Maybe it's a secret code," said Poppy, puzzling over the plants. "Or maybe whoever is in the Dark House is taking plants from the garden."

"Or even planting them," said KC. "We just don't know!"

Poppy and Sam said goodbye to Jess and KC.

"And another thing," said Poppy to Sam, as they went to eat. "We have to find Nicholas. I've got a few questions I want to ask him!"

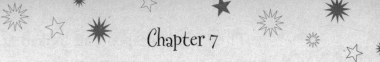

Chapter 7

A Walk in the Woods

KC rode her bike over early the next morning. "We don't have to look for Nicholas," she said when Poppy opened the door. "He's already here!" KC put her bike in the back garden, and they all rushed out to see him.

Nicholas didn't look very happy. He was standing outside Mrs. Linder's house, with the big pair of binoculars around his neck. Mrs. Linder was standing on her porch, talking to him. Even before the three friends walked over to them, they could see that Mrs. Linder looked very angry.

"How dare you go into someone else's house!" she said sternly. "Entering property that doesn't belong to you!"

Nicholas stood there, hanging his head. Poppy rushed up to him. "What do you mean, Mrs. Linder?" she asked.

"This boy is the one going into Mr. Faltermeyer's house!" Mrs. Linder replied.

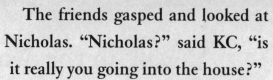

The friends gasped and looked at Nicholas. "Nicholas?" said KC, "is it really you going into the house?"

Nicholas shook his head. "No! Really, it's not! I don't know what she's talking about!"

Mrs. Linder shook her head. "Ridiculous," she said. She pointed to a faded red flower Nicholas had twined around the binoculars. "That's all the proof I need. Taking flowers out of someone else's garden! If I see you around here again, I'm going to call your parents!"

Nicholas looked horrified. "Don't do that," he pleaded. "Please, I've done nothing wrong!"

"Mrs. Linder, it can't be true," said Poppy. "We know Nicholas, and he would never do something like that."

Mrs. Linder grunted. "I've warned you. Stay off other people's property!" She went back into the house and banged the door shut. Nicholas, Poppy, KC and Sam were left standing outside with dazed looks on their faces. Nicholas stared at them, but didn't say anything. He looked totally miserable.

Poppy wanted to ask Nicholas lots of questions about the house, and where he'd been, and whether he was the one they'd seen yesterday afternoon. But she didn't. "Come on," she said. "Come inside and tell us what happened."

They sat down at the kitchen table and asked Poppy's mum for some juice and biscuits. Nicholas looked a lot happier after his second biscuit. He took his matchbox out of his pocket and put a crumb in it, for Edgar the spider.

"Who is she?" Nicholas asked. "And why did she say I was in some Dark House?"

The friends told him about the mystery, and the strange person they'd glimpsed but never managed to catch.

"It can't be me," he said. "You said that boy had a bike? I don't even have a bike!"

That made Poppy, KC and Sam feel much better. "I'm sorry we mentioned you to Mrs. Linder," said Poppy. "I just said you were walking by. I never thought she would think you were the one in the house!"

"That's okay, Poppy," said Nicholas. "It's not your fault!"

"But you mentioned a secret," Poppy said. "Something you couldn't tell us. You mean that wasn't about the Dark House at all?"

Nicholas shook his head solemnly and took another biscuit. He looked at the three friends, as if he was trying to make his mind up. "Okay," he said. "You guys stuck up for me when that woman called me a trespasser. So I'll tell you my secret. Can we go for a walk?"

Poppy, KC and Sam followed Nicholas down the road. "Your street is the only way I know to get to the woods," he said. "That's why I was passing today. And the day before yesterday, too."

The three friends knew the woods very well. They weren't far from Poppy's house, so they visited whenever they could.

It was a perfect day. Although the air was cool, the sky was clear and everything seemed to glow. The wood was at the bottom of the hill. They followed the path down to where the trees started to close in.

"We have to get to the other side of the woods," said Nicholas.

"Then we should just follow the path through the woods," said Poppy.

Nicholas smiled. "Maybe not," he said and walked on. The path bent round, and Nicholas was hidden behind a large oak tree. The three friends went around it, but Nicholas was suddenly nowhere to be seen.

"Where did he go?" asked KC. "He was just here."

"I still am!" Nicholas's voice came from behind them. He was looking out of a small gap in the trees. "Follow me!"

Poppy, KC and Sam moved in between the trees. Nicholas was waiting for them on a small path that wound its way through the trees. They formed a sort of tunnel overhead.

"It's a shortcut!" said Nicholas. "I found it, and nobody else knows about it but me!"

The friends followed Nicholas along the path. "I thought I knew all the paths in the wood," said Poppy, "But this is new to me!" But as she walked down the path, she still couldn't get the Dark House out of her mind. If it wasn't Nicholas, who was the strange person they had seen? Was it someone they had already met?

The path went downhill until it reached a small clearing. "I know where we are," said KC. "This is the other side of the wood, and that's the regular path over there!"

"Great, isn't it?" said Nicholas. He pointed to some colourful red flowers in the undergrowth. "I always pick a bunch of these poppies to take to my mum."

"That's what made Mrs. Linder think you were in the Dark House!" said KC.

Nicholas put his fingers to his lips. "Shhh. You all have to be very quiet now."

Nicholas tiptoed over to a tree with lots of wide, low branches. He started to climb up, and the others followed him. They soon sat on a wide branch, not too high off of the ground. Nicholas pointed to a tree opposite them. "Can you see?"

Poppy looked over and saw a small nest of twigs in one of the branches. As she watched, a grey-winged bird settled on the nest.

"So that's your secret!" whispered Poppy. "You've been watching a bird's nest!"

"Yes," said Nicholas. "Watch that bird. He's got worms for the babies." And sure enough, three tiny mouths emerged from the nest, and the adult bird fed them all.

Nicholas was looking through his binoculars. "I can see the chicks really clearly with this," said Nicholas softly. "They've been here for a week now. I didn't tell anyone. I didn't want anyone spoiling it, or making too much noise for the grown-up birds to come back. So, you see," he said, looking at the three friends, "I had to keep it a secret."

"We understand, Nicholas," said KC. "We won't tell anyone else, either."

Nicholas passed around the binoculars and they all watched the birds. It was easier than using the telescope, Poppy decided. And what she could see was much nicer, too. As she was focusing the binoculars, another bird fluttered onto the nest.

"That's the mother bird, I think," said Nicholas. "Those chicks always seem to need feeding!" But he said it very quietly, so as not to scare the birds.

It was peaceful to sit up in the tree, in the quiet woods, and watch the birds. Both birds kept returning to the nest with more worms and insects. "Don't worry, Edgar," Nicholas whispered into Edgar's matchbox. "I won't let them feed you to the chicks!"

Sam had brought his camera along, and he took a few photos of the tree and its chicks. "I need one of those big zoom lenses to get a proper picture," he muttered.

After half an hour of watching, Poppy, KC and Sam walked back up the shortcut with Nicholas. "I knew it wasn't you, Nicholas," said KC.

"Who wants to go into a house anyway, when you could be in the woods?" Nicholas said.

Poppy was thinking hard. "Well, someone does. And we're still no nearer to finding it out. First of all, we need to tell Mrs. Linder that it's not you!"

Chapter 8

The Attic Disappearance

When Poppy, KC, Sam and Nicholas got back to Poppy's street, they knocked on Mrs. Linder's door. Nicholas looked nervous, but determined. Mrs. Linder opened the door. "Oh it's you, Poppy, and KC, and Sam, and you." She frowned at Nicholas. "I thought I told you not to come back to that house!"

Poppy interrupted. "Please, Mrs. Linder. Nicholas found a bird's nest in the woods, and he wasn't . . ."

"I don't want to hear any more!" said Mrs. Linder. "I'm calling your parents, Nicholas!"

Nicholas looked shocked. "But, Mrs. Linder," KC started, but Mrs. Linder was already starting to close the door.

"You owe me one," whispered Sam to Nicholas.

"What for?" said Nicholas.

"This," said Sam. He rushed up to Mrs. Linder and pretended to cry.

"My-hy-hy friend!" Sam said. "He's so-ho-ho

so-ho-rry! Please," Sam said, hugging Mrs. Linder hard, "Please don't phone his mum and da-ha-ha-ad!"

Mrs. Linder's face softened, as she hugged Sam. "There, there," she said. "Don't cry."

"I got pho-ho-tos of the birds," said Sam, trying to pretend to cry and show her the bird photos at the same time. "Look! I mean, loo-hoo-hoo-ook!" He held them up on his camera, but Mrs. Linder wasn't really looking.

"I suppose his story might be true," and she looked down at Sam, who was rubbing his eyes to try and make tears come out.

Nicholas looked relieved, but Mrs. Linder continued. "I'll give you until tomorrow night to prove he's innocent. If not, I'm calling his parents!" Her eyes flashed, and she closed the door.

Sam made a face.

Nicholas smiled at him. "Thanks, Sam."

Sam smiled back. "That's okay. It was worth it, to see the birds."

"Okay," said Poppy. "We have one day to find out who is really in the house!"

Poppy, KC, Sam and Nicholas were back in Poppy's bedroom. Suddenly, the mystery of the Dark House didn't just seem important to the three friends. Now, it was important to Nicholas, too.

"Maybe we can find more clues in the attic," said KC. "We didn't get to see it after the person climbed up."

"Good thinking, KC," said Poppy. They went upstairs with the torch. Sam looked through the window with the telescope, before Poppy switched on the torch.

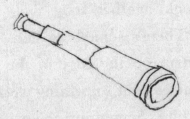

"I can't see anything!" said Sam.

"What do you mean?" asked KC. "Is the lens cap on the telescope?"

Sam looked puzzled. "I can just about see into the attic - but I don't think there's anything there!"

Poppy took her turn as KC shone the light into the attic of the Dark House.

"Sam's right!" Poppy could see into the attic, all right. But it was bare. There were no books or magazines, and the chair was gone. It was as if they had never been in there in the first place.

KC took a look. "How could they have all gone?" she asked. "Do you think the person in the Dark House has gone for good?"

"Maybe," said Poppy.

"But that means we'll never find out who it was," said Sam. "And we'll never be able to prove that it wasn't Nicholas!"

Poppy took another long look through the telescope. "There's something here, still." When she zoomed in on the edge of the window, she could see the edge of something wooden. It was a pale, faded blue. Something about it was familiar to Poppy. She tried hard to think of where she had seen the same thing.

"I know!" Poppy said. "That's the chair!"

"So it is still up there?" asked KC.

"Right," Poppy said. "Which means that whoever was in the attic before, has moved everything! They've shifted everything away from the window, so we can't see it. I bet the books are all up there, too!"

"Whatever," said Sam. "It's no good if we can't see him any more!" He looked through the telescope. "You know what? He might be in there right now, laughing at us!"

Poppy's sharp eyes caught a glimpse of movement. But it wasn't coming from the attic. It was someone outside, in the garden. "Quick!" she called. "Someone's down there!"

Chapter 9

Someone in the Garden

They rushed back downstairs, past Poppy's mum, right into the back garden, and crawled under the hedge.

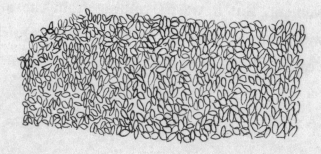

"Where did you go?" called Nicholas. He had been slower than Poppy, KC and Sam. But there was no time to explain. They were already on the other side of the fence.

"Spread out!" whispered Poppy. "Whoever it is must be out here somewhere."

It had happened so quickly that KC hadn't had time to feel scared. She ran off on her own, checking the overgrown flowerbeds.

"What if we do find someone?" KC thought.

"What do we say to them?"

But there was no sign of anyone hiding among the flowers.

Sam went straight to the back of the garden. "Poppy," he called out in a low voice. "It's a waste of time. There's nobody he-eeaaargh!" Sam had just seen someone staring at him from up in the tree!

Sam wanted to turn and run, but managed to stop himself in time. He didn't want to look like a baby in front of Poppy and KC. He looked up the tree again, and saw who it was. "Jess!" he called. "What are you doing here?"

Jess was clinging onto a branch. "Sam! You scared me! I thought it was someone from the Dark House!"

Poppy and KC ran up to the tree. "Trying to scare us again, Jess?" said Poppy.

"No, honestly," said Jess. "I wanted to find out who was in the house. So I came in through the side gate that leads to the garden. You know, to look for clues, like you all do. But I didn't find anything."

"It must have been you we saw in the garden," sighed Poppy. "Not the mysterious person. Did you leave the gate open?"

"Yes," said Jess. "Why?"

"Because," said Poppy, "anyone looking from the street can see the gate. So if someone sees it's open, they might come to investigate."

"No way," said Jess. "We're fine in here. I don't think anyone will . . ."

At that moment, they heard a squeaking and slamming. It was the gate from the front of the house being pushed back!

"Quick!" called Poppy. "Into the tree!"

They all quickly scrambled up near Jess. In a moment, they were all hidden, except Sam couldn't reach the branch. They could hear someone moving past the junk in the alley.

"Help!" said Sam.

Jess reached down and helped to pull him up. His feet disappeared into the tree. Seconds later, someone was in the garden.

"Mrs. Linder!" said Poppy. "I knew she'd spot the open gate!"

Poppy peeked through the leaves to see what she was doing. "If Mrs. Linder catches us here, she'll think it's us inside the house for sure!"

Mrs. Linder was walking around the garden. First, she looked into the Dark House through the kitchen window. Then she went and examined the statue of the winged child.

"She's probably going to tell the statue off for trespassing," giggled Jess.

"Shhh!" said Poppy, KC and Sam, making more noise than Jess had. Mrs. Linder seemed to hear something. She tramped to the back of the garden and stood underneath the trees. Poppy, KC, Sam and Jess tried to stay as still as they could. If Mrs. Linder looked up, she'd see them.

Then they heard a noise. "Poppy," Nicholas was calling over the fence. "Where are you?"

"That boy!" said Mrs. Linder. "I knew it!"

Luckily, Nicholas didn't call out again.

Mrs. Linder looked everywhere, but couldn't find any trace of Nicholas. She didn't see the hole in the fence, either. Poppy was very glad Nicholas hadn't seen it, either, because if he had, he'd have tried to come through.

"There's no room on this branch," whispered KC. "I'm going to fall off soon!"

The branch wasn't very big, and it was hard to hold onto it. At last, Mrs. Linder seemed to give up. She went back to the alley that led to the front of the house, grumbling all the way. Just as they heard the gate slam shut, KC felt herself slipping. She slid down the trunk of the tree to the ground.

"Phew," said KC. "That was close!"

They heard a dinging sound from the house. "Mrs. Linder must be ringing the doorbell," said Poppy. "Let's go!"

They crawled back through the hole, surprising Nicholas. "There you are!" he said. "Who's that?" Jess had come back through with them.

Poppy explained what had happened.

"That ringing must be scaring whoever's in the house," said Jess.

They went back inside Poppy and Sam's house, and peeped out of the front window. Nobody had answered the doorbell of the Dark House. Mrs. Linder walked back across the street to her own house, looking annoyed.

"Wait a minute," said Poppy. Things were coming together in her head. "That gives me an idea. If someone is in the Dark House right now, I think I have a plan to find out who it is, once and for all. Listen!"

KC, Jess, Nicholas and Sam huddled around her, and she told them what to do.

Chapter 10

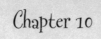

Poppy's Big Plan

The first part of the plan was easy. Jess went to get her walkie-talkies. When she brought them back, they went up to the attic bedroom.

Poppy explained the next step.

"It's tricky," Jess said, "But it might just work!"

Jess handed a walkie-talkie to Nicholas. "Are you sure you know how to use one of these?"

Nicholas saluted. "Yes!"

Jess took up her position at the telescope.

Nicholas went downstairs to the spare bedroom. From there, he could see into the back garden of the Dark House through the window.

Poppy, KC and Sam went to the back garden, to collect what they needed. It took a while for them to get ready. Nicholas could see them in the alley that led from the front of Poppy's house to the back.

"You okay?" Poppy asked KC and Sam.

"Yes," said KC, looking excited.

"Yes," said Sam, looking determined.

Poppy gave Nicholas the thumbs-up through the window. It was the signal to start Poppy's plan. There was no turning back.

Nicholas pressed the button on the walkie-talkie. "Jess, can you hear me?"

"Yes," said Jess's crackly voice, over the walkie-talkie.

"Poppy, KC and Sam are ready," he spoke into the device.

"You have to say 'over' when you've finished speaking on a walkie-talkie, over," said Jess.

"Sorry! I mean, Poppy, KC and Sam are ready, over," said Nicholas.

"That's better," said Jess.

"Don't you mean 'That's better, over', over?" asked Nicholas.

"Be quiet, over," said Jess, trying not to laugh. "This is very serious, over!"

Meanwhile, Poppy was walking to the front door of the Dark House. She looked at the half-open gate as she went past, the one that led to the back garden. "I hope Mrs. Linder isn't watching now," she thought.

Poppy reached up and rang the doorbell of the Dark House. From deep inside the house, Poppy could hear the low dinging sound. "What if Mr. Faltermeyer answers the door?" she thought. "What if it's him in the attic all along?" Poppy didn't like the idea of the door swinging open to see an angry man asking her what she was doing.

But nobody answered. She ran back to the alley by her house, where KC and Sam were waiting.

"All set."

"Anything happening up there?" said Nicholas into the walkie-talkie.

Jess looked through the telescope. "Someone's moving in there! He must have heard the doorbell ring again. Maybe he's getting nervous."

"Great! Now switch the torch on," said Nicholas.

"I am!" said Jess, and switched it on. Looking through the telescope, she could see that someone had moved to the window. She shone the torch, and waved it around as much as she could. The person dashed down the trapdoor and back into the house.

"He's out, over!" Jess called into the walkie-talkie.

Nicholas heard, and signalled to Poppy, KC and Sam through the window. Then he turned to watch the back garden of the Dark House. He saw the kitchen door open, and someone dash around the corner, into the alley.

Nicholas signalled to Poppy, KC and Sam again, and they moved out.

Seconds later, a bike came racing out of the alley of the Dark House. But, this time, Poppy, KC and Sam were ready for them!

They were waiting in the street on their bikes. As the mysterious biker zoomed past them, they were already pedaling. This time, when the bike turned the corner, they were right behind it.

"It worked!" Poppy shouted as they raced down the road. "Ringing the bell and flashing the light scared the person out of the house."

"Poppy, what's the next part of the plan?" called KC.

"Um, this!" said Poppy, as they skidded around another corner. "I didn't think he'd be this quick!"

The bike whizzed around another corner, and they followed. "We need to find out the truth from that boy," Poppy said.

But the boy on the bike was a fast rider. They saw his face turn to look at them from the bike, and he put on a burst of speed.

"He knows we're following him!" said KC.

He turned sharply, and headed down an alley. Poppy, KC and Sam couldn't make the turn in time. A high wall separated them from the mystery biker.

"Is he getting away?" Sam asked worriedly, pedaling as fast as he could.

Poppy stood up on her pedals. "I can still see him over the fence! Quick!"

Poppy was going as fast as she could, but it was no good. The boy was still pulling further and further away. He came out of the alley and turned right in front of them, pedaling uphill now.

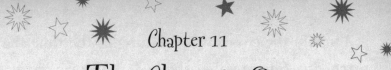

Chapter 11

The Chase is On

Even though Poppy, KC and Sam pushed as hard as they could, the mysterious biker reached the top of the hill way before them.

"We'll ... never ... catch ... up," panted KC.

"Don't give up!" said Poppy, straining at the pedals. "We're nearly at the top!" But Poppy realised that there wasn't much chance of catching up now. She knew that when they reached the top of the hill, the boy on the bike would probably be right at the bottom, on the other side.

Poppy stopped at the top of the hill and looked down. The boy on the bike was still in front of them, but there was a crowd of people on the pavement. The biker was having to dodge past them. The three friends saw the biker look up at them, and then he got off his bike and started to wheel it through the crowd.

"We still have a chance!" called Poppy, and set off down the hill.

71

Luckily, the crowd was thinning by the time she reached it. She saw that she had almost caught up with the cyclist. KC and Sam weren't far behind.

They saw that someone else was running out of the crowd, towards the biker. Poppy realised that it was the older girl they had seen outside the Dark House. Poppy whizzed right past the girl, wishing she had time to stop and ask her some questions. "Why was she outside the Dark House?" Poppy wondered. "Does she know what's going on inside?"

The girl saw Poppy and looked at her in surprise, but Poppy zoomed past her. In fact, Poppy was starting to catch up with the cyclist. She looked behind them after some frantic pedaling, and saw that the girl had given up the chase.

KC and Sam were right behind her. "This guy can't go on forever," said KC.

"Neither can I!" puffed Sam. They followed the cyclist all the way down the other side of the hill. Then the boy turned back towards Poppy's street.

"I wish we knew where he was going!" said Sam.

"I thinks he's heading into the woods," said

Poppy. "We have to catch up with him, or we'll lose him again!"

But by the time the three friends had reached the wood, the biker had disappeared into the darkness of the trees. They cycled in. The path was uneven. Roots, twigs and stones lay on the ground. It took longer to ride over everything. None of them wanted to fall off.

"He'll have gone all the way around the wood by now," KC said, coming to a halt. "There's no way we can catch him." She leaned against a big oak and got her breath back.

Poppy stared at the oak. "I remember this tree." She wheeled her bike around and disappeared into the trees.

For a moment, KC and Sam were stunned. And then they remembered.

"Nicholas's shortcut!" they said together, and pulled their bikes around to follow Poppy.

The secret path was very narrow. The branches seemed to pull at them from both sides. They tried to stick right to the middle of the path. Soon, they were riding downhill. It seemed a lot steeper than the last time they were here, now they were on bikes. KC held down the brakes as she inched forward. Sam nearly went into a skid before he managed to stop. Poppy controlled her speed and made her way carefully down the path. She emerged into the small clearing, near to the tree that held the bird's nest. There was nobody there.

"Did we miss him?" she wondered, as KC and Sam cycled out of the gap in the trees. "He can't be that fast. Can he?"

A few seconds later, she got her answer. The bike was heading towards them, out of the main path. Its rider wasn't pedaling as fast any more.

"There he is!" said Poppy. "He thinks he's got away!"

The rider didn't see them until he was almost in the clearing. He braked sharply, sending his bike into a wide skid. But he was too skillful to fall over. He stopped the bike just before he got to a tree, and stood looking at them. He wiped his forehead. The friends could see he was just as worn out as they were; maybe even more so.

The boy was wearing a big, puffy coat, and had short, bright blond hair. He didn't move for a second or two.

"Is he going to ride off again?" Poppy thought. "We'll never catch him if he does!"

But the boy got off his bike and sat down next to the tree.

"Phew!" he said. "How did you get here so quickly?"

"That's a secret," Poppy said. "We'll tell you, if you tell us yours!"

The boy looked up at her and frowned. "Secret?" he said. "What secret?"

Poppy, KC and Sam walked up to him, and sat down. "We know where you were," Poppy said. "We saw you in the Dark House!"

The boy looked worried, and then a crafty look settled on his face. "So?" he asked. "So what?"

"So, we know you shouldn't be in there," KC replied. "It belongs to Mr. Faltermeyer!"

The boy looked at the three friends. He laughed. "I know that," he said. "I know Mr. Faltermeyer!"

Chapter 12

Zach and the Potions

"You know Mr. Faltermeyer?" asked Sam, in astonishment.

"Yes." The boy continued, "My name's Zach. Mr. Faltermeyer is my uncle! I come over to visit him sometimes." He shrugged.

Poppy looked at Zach closely. She couldn't tell if he was telling the truth or not. He stared back at her. He didn't seem angry, or moody. And he didn't look scared or worried, either.

"Mr. Faltermeyer gives me errands to run," he explained. "Go there, bring this, do that. I'm busy."

Poppy thought hard. "If Mr. Faltermeyer is in the house, why is it dark all the time?"

Zach shrugged again. "I guess he likes it dark. He's a little strange."

KC couldn't contain her curiosity. "What's he like?"

Zach looked at her and raised his eyebrows. "Scary. He wears really weird clothes. He carries a stick, and you can hear it tapping all over the house. When he gets nearer the tapping gets louder... tap... tap... TAP!" He shouted the last word, and the friends drew back a little.

Poppy thought hard again. "We saw some words in a notebook," she said. "Rowan, ash, lily, rose. What do all those plants mean?"

When Poppy mentioned the plants, she saw Zach's face freeze. But then he laughed, and said, "They're ingredients in his potions."

This sounded interesting. "Potions?" asked Poppy.

"Yes. He makes all kinds of stuff, in the basement, where you can't see it. I go out into the garden, and collect everything. Then Mr. Faltermeyer brews it and drinks it. Says it keeps him strong. It smells awful," said Zach, wrinkling his nose.

The friends thought about what Zach had said. "I'm Poppy," said Poppy. "This is KC, and this is Sam. We live next door to the Dark - that is, next door to Mr. Faltermeyer's house."

Zach looked at them. He laughed a little. "Poppy? Did you say Poppy?"

"Have you heard of me before?" asked Poppy.

"No," said Zach, "It's just a funny name!" Before Poppy could reply, Zach continued. "So you're the ones, hmmm? Mr. Faltermeyer said he'd seen you spying on him!"

The friends were aghast. "We didn't know!" said Poppy. "We didn't think it was him in the house."

Zach got to his feet and picked up his bike. He got on it, and said, "You should leave him alone. He doesn't like people prying!"

With those words, Zach started to pedal off. In a few moments, he was out of sight, down the path.

"Weirder and weirder," said Poppy.

"Mr. Faltermeyer sounds scary," said KC.

"Hmm," said Poppy. "A little too scary, if you ask me."

"What do you mean?" asked Sam.

"I don't know just yet," said Poppy. "But I'm not sure Zach was telling the truth."

"And what's so funny about the name Poppy, anyway?" asked KC. "It's a lovely name!"

Poppy got on her bike and checked her helmet. "Let's go home. We have some more investigating to do!"

On the way back, Sam and KC talked about the odd-sounding man and his potions.

"He's so weird, he makes Mrs. Linder look normal!" said Sam.

Poppy was quiet. She was thinking hard. When they got back, she made them stop at Mrs. Linder's house, and knocked on the door. But there was no answer.

"Good," said Sam.

But Poppy looked frustrated. "We have to speak to her," she said.

"I don't understand," said KC. "Why now?"

"Because of Nicholas!" said Poppy. "If we don't tell Mrs. Linder about Zach, she's going to get Nicholas in big trouble tomorrow!"

But it was no use. Mrs. Linder was out, and

Nicholas and Jess had gone home. Poppy and Sam said goodbye to KC and headed home.

"Do you think Mrs. Linder will believe us about Zach?" said Sam. "She didn't believe us before when we said Nicholas was innocent."

Poppy found a big book of plants, and leafed through it on the bed. There was rowan, a tree with bright red berries. There was ash, a taller tree with thin leaves. She turned the pages and saw the lily, with its big, beautiful petals. And there was a deep red rose. But what was so important about these four plants? And why had Zach looked so worried for a moment when Poppy had mentioned them?

"There must be a reason," Poppy thought. But try as she might, she couldn't think what they could mean. She asked Sam to look up the plants on the computer, to find out if there was any information about them on the internet.

Sam typed on the keyboard. "Don't know. Can't find anything about potions. Wait. People used to say ash kept snakes away, and rowan protected you from evil."

"What about lilies and roses?" asked Poppy.

"It says here that lilies can mean tenderness. Red roses mean 'I love you', eurgh. Sappy."

lily leaf

rose leaf

Poppy looked at the pictures in the book again, but they didn't help.

"Here's something," said Sam. "People used to think the ash and the rowan were related, but now they think the rowan is actually closer to the rose.

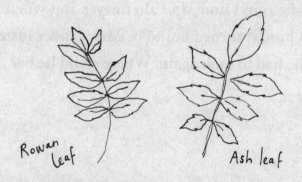

Rowan leaf

Ash leaf

What do you think that means?"

"I don't know," said Poppy. "I guess I didn't even know plants were related to one another!" That thought almost sparked off an idea in Poppy's mind. But then it faded, as ideas sometimes do. "Probably nothing," Poppy said to herself.

Poppy lay on her bed, trying to think straight. But so many pictures kept whirling through her mind: Zach on his bike, Nicholas in trouble, Jess with her telescope, the man brewing potions in his basement - what was true, and what wasn't? How could she find out?

When Poppy fell asleep, she had a strange dream. She was in a computer game like MegaRobots, but it was set in the Dark House. She had to run around the house, gathering clues to save Nicholas, until she could find Mr. Faltermeyer. But when she found him, it turned out to be Mrs. Linder instead, and she had to look again. Where could he be?

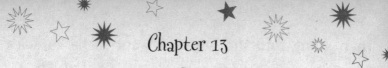

Chapter 13

Rowan, Ash, Lily, Rose

When Poppy woke up, she knew what she had to do. She had to go see Mrs. Linder. After breakfast, she asked Sam to come with her.

He shook his head. "No way, Poppy."

"Okay," smiled Poppy. "I'll go by myself." She picked up her blue rucksack and ran over to Mrs. Linder's house. It was a foggy morning. The trees dripped with moisture, and the houses down the street seemed to be hiding in clouds. Even the everyday sounds of cars and birds seemed fuzzy.

Mrs. Linder was home. She looked at Poppy suspiciously. "What is it, Poppy? Is that boy Nicholas back again?"

Poppy felt a little nervous. She wished KC and Sam were with her. But she knew what she had to ask. "Mrs. Linder," said Poppy, "Do you have any pictures of Mr. Faltermeyer?"

"Why do you want them?" Mrs. Linder asked her.

Poppy was ready for this question. "If we see a

man going into the house, I want to be sure it's Mr. Faltermeyer, so we don't call the police," she answered. "Well, it's true," she thought to herself. "Even if it isn't the real reason."

Mrs. Linder invited Poppy into her living room and pulled out a big photo album. It was so old, Poppy half-expected the pictures to be in black and white.

"I don't know," said Mrs. Linder, looking through the album. "Maybe there's one here, from before we stopped talking to each other." She pointed to an old photo of her and a friend smiling at the camera. "He came to a party at my house, once. Yes, I think that's Mr. Faltermeyer, in the background."

The background was out of focus, but she could see a man's head and his face. It was hard to tell what he looked like because he was turning away from the camera, but Poppy could see enough.

Poppy's eyes lit up. "I knew it!" she said.

Mrs. Linder was surprised. "What do you know? What's in the picture that's so strange?"

But Poppy was already leaving. "Thanks, Mrs. Linder!"

Mrs. Linder shut the door and frowned. "What a

strange girl," she said.

KC and Nicholas were there when Poppy got back home.

"Quick," she said, "Let's go into the garden. I've got something to tell you!" Poppy grabbed her plant book, and they all dashed out back. It was still very foggy, and they couldn't help looking up at the Dark House as they sat down at a picnic table. The house seemed quiet, but was Mr. Faltermeyer in there right now? Was he ordering Zach to collect the four plants from the garden, to brew into a strange potion?

"We have to go back into the garden of the Dark House," said Poppy. "We said we were going to look for the plants in the book. But then we saw Nicholas, and he showed us the bird's nest, and we forgot! Come on!"

"Do you know something, Poppy?" asked KC. "Something about the mystery?"

"I think so," said Poppy. "And I'm going to find out!" She pushed through the hedge and went through the hole.

Sam, Nicholas and KC got down on all fours. "But Poppy," called KC, "what if Mr. Faltermeyer sees us?"

"If I'm right," said Poppy, "he won't!" And she wouldn't say any more than that.

The others climbed through. It was cold and damp, and the garden was cloaked in mist.

Poppy showed them the plant book. "We need to look for these. Sam, check for ash trees. KC, look for roses. Nicholas, try to find lilies. I'll look for rowan trees."

Sam looked up at the trees. They seemed to bend over to look back at him. He tried to forget about the windows of the Dark House that looked onto the garden. He tried not to think about someone looking down at them, starting to make their way slowly down the stairs towards the back door, tapping all the way.

KC examined all the borders for flowers. It was hard to tell what plants they were. Most of them were overgrown, and the flowers that were on them were old and wilting. She tried not to think about the gloomy corridors inside the house, and the kitchen door that led to them. KC didn't like the dark at all.

Poppy called them together in the centre of the

garden. "Are there ash trees in the garden, Sam?"

Sam shook his head. "All these trees are oaks. You can tell, because all the leaves are wiggly around the edges. There aren't any other trees in the garden at all!"

Poppy didn't look upset. In fact, she looked pleased.

"Did you find any lilies, Nicholas?"

Nicholas shook his head.

"How about you, KC?"

"No," KC said. "There are some flowers, but no roses. I found this, though!" She showed Poppy a red flower with a small black centre. "It's a poppy! Just like you!" She tucked it into Poppy's jet-black hair.

Poppy smiled. Then she looked thoughtful. "That reminds me," she said. She was about to continue, when ...

"Help!"

It was a small voice, and they couldn't see where it was coming from.

"Help!"

Chapter 14

Inside the Dark House

The friends spun around. "Jess?" said Poppy. "Is that you again?"

But it didn't sound like Jess. It didn't sound very spooky, either. It just sounded like someone in trouble.

The cry came again. The friends realised that it was coming from inside the Dark House.

"What do we do?" asked Sam. "It definitely came from in there!" He pointed to the kitchen door.

"There's no time," said Poppy. "We have to go in!" She marched through the long grass to the kitchen door, and tried the handle. It turned easily.

KC and Sam rushed up, but hesitated at the door.

"Poppy," said KC, "You know we're not allowed to go inside the house. Your mum and dad said so."

"I know," said Poppy, "But someone in there

needs our help. Nicholas, you go tell someone. We're going in!"

Sam looked at Poppy, frowning. "You're right," he said at last. "Let's go."

KC looked up at the Dark House. "Okay. But let's get in, help the person, and get out again as quickly as we can!"

Poppy opened the door, and the three friends finally stepped inside the Dark House. "At least it's not too dark in here," said KC, trying to sound cheerful. Grey light from the foggy day came in through the big window. Now they were inside, the three friends felt a lot braver. After all, the empty kitchen wasn't exactly scary. In fact, it looked very clean. Poppy ran her fingers down one side of a cupboard. "Strange," she said. "When we looked in before, this kitchen was dusty."

They heard the voice again. "Can anyone hear me? Help!" It was definitely coming from inside the house.

Sam grabbed Poppy's arm. "Poppy! What if it's a trap?"

But Poppy was intrigued. She shook her head.

She left the kitchen, and went into the gloomy hallway.

Even KC could see that it wasn't really dark in the Dark House. At least, not during the daytime. Once her eyes got used to the gloom, she found she could see quite clearly. The Dark House really seemed empty. There was no sound of tapping, or bubbling potions.

They looked into the rooms at the front of the house. There was still some furniture. The heavy curtains blocked out most of the light, though. Turning back, Poppy noticed a green door in the hallway. "That door must lead down to the basement," KC said. "That's where Zach, the kid on the bike, said Mr. Faltermeyer brews his potions!"

"You don't think he's in here, do you Poppy?" Sam asked nervously.

Poppy squeezed his hand. "No, I don't," said Poppy. "We'll be okay."

"How can you know?" asked Sam.

But Poppy was already climbing the stairs. "I'll tell you later!"

She stopped halfway up the stairs. Now they could hear a strange knocking sound. And it seemed to be coming from the ceiling above them.

Poppy reached the top of the stairs and looked around. Closed doors seemed to lead off in all directions. But it looked very familiar, somehow. Why?

"Zach, is that you?" called Poppy. It sounded like the strange boy on the bike.

A faint voice came down to her. "Poppy?"

"Zach! What's happened? Are you okay?"

"I'm fine," said Zach. "I'm in the attic! I'm stuck up here," called Zach through the ceiling. "There's a hatch. Can you find it?"

Poppy looked at the ceiling of the landing. No hatch.

Suddenly, everything slotted together in Poppy's head. "Of course!" she said. "That's why the inside of the Dark House looks so familiar! It's exactly like our house!"

Poppy looked around. It was as if she was seeing everything for the first time. "Sam, that door leads to your bedroom, and that's the bathroom, that must be Mum and Dad's room!"

"Yes," said Sam, "I get it. Poppy, if that's right, then we know where the hatch is."

"The spare room!" said Poppy and Sam at the same time. It was where the stairs to the attic room were, in their house.

Poppy tried the door. It was locked. "Zach must have locked it behind him," said Poppy. "He didn't know he'd get stuck in the attic."

Poppy thought hard, and looked around. The room through this door was the same as the spare room. There was no other way in. But there was another little room next to the spare room. It was a small private shower room for guests. And it backed on to where Poppy's room should be.

Poppy tried the next door down. This was her room, in her house. Aha! This door opened. It led into another empty room, the same size and shape as Poppy's, but totally empty.

Poppy knew that when the shower ran in her

parents' shower room, she could hear it through the wall. She remembered what her dad had said about it once: "It's not a solid wall, Poppy. If you wanted, you could break through and take a shower!"

Poppy knocked on the wall that separated this room from the shower room. She knew that you could hear when a wall wasn't solid. And, sure enough, when she knocked on one section, it made a hollow sound. In fact, a whole panel of the wall itself felt bendy. It was just a thin panel, painted white!

Poppy called, "Sam, do you have your screwdriver?"

Sam almost always carried a tiny screwdriver in a pocket. "Sometimes, I need it," he said when Poppy and her parents laughed. And this was one of those times.

Poppy used the screwdriver to push open the panel in the wall. It slid up neatly, leaving a hole just big enough to crawl through.

"Great work, Poppy!" KC grinned, and all three of them went through the hole. Poppy carefully closed the panel behind her.

Now they were in a tiny room with a shower and toilet. Poppy tried the door. This one opened, too. It led to the locked room. "The spare room," Poppy said to herself. In one corner, there was a stepladder that led to a hatch in the ceiling. But the hatch was shut. Poppy climbed the stepladder and pushed on the hatch door. It wouldn't open.

"It's stuck," said Zach, mournfully, from the other side. "That's why I called for help. Poppy, can you open it?"

Poppy pushed with all her strength, but the door wouldn't budge. Poppy called KC to help. KC stood on the stepladder, one step behind Poppy. It was tricky for KC to balance and push on the door at the same time, but she tried. Poppy and KC both pushed as hard as they could, but nothing happened.

Sam got onto the step

below KC. The stepladder creaked. It wasn't meant to have three people on it at once, even if they were small. "I can just reach," said Sam, standing on tiptoe and pushing.

Crack! The hatch door flew upwards, slamming into the attic floor above. Poppy, KC and Sam almost lost their balance for a second. Poppy grabbed onto the open hatch, KC grabbed onto Poppy, and Sam grabbed onto KC. After a moment, they all got their balance back. And then the three friends climbed up into the attic.

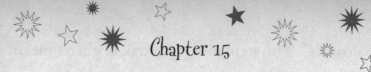

Chapter 15

Answers in the Attic

A torch light shone in their faces and, behind it, they saw Zach, the boy that had led them such a long chase the day before. It seemed like ages ago now. This time, he didn't look so sly. In fact, he looked really pleased to see them.

"Oh, thanks!" said Zach. "Thank you so much! You three really are detectives, aren't you?"

As Zach swung his torch around, the friends could see the attic clearly for the first time. The floor was covered with wide boards. In between the boards, you could see down to the rafters. On the biggest board, away from the window, sat the blue chair they had seen through the telescope. It had been moved away from the window, just as they had thought. The chair was surrounded by books and magazines. Poppy noticed the notebook with the plant names, too.

Zach looked at them closely. "Weren't you worried that Mr. Faltermeyer would come and get you? I thought he would scare you off."

"No," said Poppy. "Because I know Mr. Faltermeyer isn't here. And he hasn't been here all this time, either."

KC and Sam gasped. Zach looked surprised.

Poppy looked at him. "Has he, Zach?"

Zach looked sly again for a second, and then he shrugged. "You're right, Poppy," he said. "Mr. Faltermeyer isn't here. But how did you know?"

Poppy sat down on the chair. "Mrs. Linder showed me a picture of Mr. Faltermeyer. He was happy and smiling – not frowning or angry-looking at all. Not strange, or scary, the way you'd described him. And you also said that you went to pick those plants from outside – rowan, ash, lily and rose."

"And we just found out that none of them are out there," said KC. "Right! So you must have been making that up, too."

"I don't get it," said Sam. "What are those names of plants for, then?"

Zach looked at Poppy. "Have you worked that out, too?" he asked, quietly.

"I think so," said Poppy. "Zach, do you have any brothers and sisters?"

Zach smiled and nodded. "Four. Three sisters, and one brother. I'm the middle one." "What are their names?" Poppy asked.

"The oldest," said Zach, "is Rowan. She's nearly fifteen. Then there's Ashley, my older brother. We call him Ash. I share a room with him. Lily is only six and little Rose is five years old."

KC and Sam looked at each other in surprise. "Those names are your brothers and sisters?" said KC.

"Tell us about it, Zach," said Poppy.

"We don't have a very big house," said Zach. "It's always busy. My grandma and grandpa live with us, too. Everyone is always rushing around, and shouting. And arguing. People storm in and out of rooms, and slam doors."

"It's never quiet," said Poppy.

"Right," Zach said. "I love to read, but it's hard to read when your big brother is bouncing up and down on your bed, and your little sisters are crying, and your big sister is playing loud music and singing into a hairbrush!"

"So you come here, instead," said Poppy. "Where it's quiet. And write about your family in your diary."

"That's it," said Zach. "My friends and I were exploring one day. We dared each other to go into the house. Everyone said a scary man called Mr. Faltermeyer used to live here. The back door was unlocked. So we just walked in. But there was nobody inside. Everyone else forgot about it, except me. When the noise got too much at home, I started coming here to read. I cleaned up a couple of the rooms. I thought nobody would ever find me," Zach finished, "until you started shining that torch into the attic! But I couldn't stay away. I really like it up here."

Suddenly, everything made perfect sense to the

three friends. Poppy was glad.

"Let's go," said Zach. "I have to be home in half an hour." They climbed back down the ladder, and Poppy shut the hatch behind them. "That's why I had to call for help. I didn't want Mum and Dad to worry about me." Zach thought for a second. "Poppy, how did you know those names were really my brothers and sisters?"

"I only just worked it out," said Poppy. "KC, when you put that poppy in my hair, and you said it had the same name as me, I thought that maybe it was the same thing with the plants! And then I remembered that you laughed at my name, Zach."

"Sorry," said Zach. "It seemed really funny at the time. You thought those names were plants, and your name was a flower, too!"

"It was a guess, really," said Poppy. "And I thought that if someone comes and spends all his time in a quiet, dark place, they probably have too much noise somewhere else. Someone with lots of brothers and sisters, maybe."

Poppy thought. "We saw an older girl outside this house. She had dark hair with a blonde streak, and a denim jacket. Was it your sister?"

Zach nodded. "Yes. That was Rowan. She came down here sometimes. I think she knew where I was going." Zach tried the locked door, and it opened straight away from the inside. "Sorry about that," he said. "I never knew it would lock behind me!"

Poppy, KC, Sam and Zach came out onto the landing once again. They were about to go downstairs, when something very strange happened.

With a clicking, popping sound, all the lights in the Dark House started to come on!

Suddenly, the friends and Zach were standing in light, coming from the lightbulb in the ceiling above them. Looking down the stairs, they saw that the hallway was lit as well.

They looked at one another. "Zach," said Poppy, "Did you do that?"

Zach gulped. "Nothing to do with me!"

They heard a noise from downstairs. It seemed to be coming from the hallway. Nervously, the friends made their way downstairs.

"It's coming from over there," said Poppy. She pointed to the basement door. As they watched, it opened, and someone stepped out.

Chapter 16

A Light in the Dark

A man was standing there, right in front of them!

For a moment, nobody moved. The man looked just as shocked as them. "You - what are you all doing in my house?" he demanded.

"Mr. Faltermeyer?" asked Poppy. He didn't look anything like they'd imagined. He was wearing a cream-coloured suit, he was tan, and he didn't look scary. And there was no sign of a walking stick.

For once, Poppy didn't know what to say.

Then Zach stepped forward. "Sir, I was in your attic. I got trapped, and these three heard me call for help. They came in to help me, even though they were very scared."

Mr. Faltermeyer looked at each of the children, very slowly.

"You rescued him, hmmm?" he said. "What were you doing in my attic?" He looked rather stern.

Zach swallowed nervously. "I'm sorry, sir. Your

back door was unlocked and I came in here."

Mr. Faltermeyer walked over to Zach and looked down at him. "Do you know how much trouble you're in?" he asked.

Zach looked down. "I know." His bottom lip trembled. "I'm so sorry."

"Wait!" Poppy said. "Mr. Faltermeyer, have you seen the other rooms?"

"Not yet," said Mr. Faltermeyer. "I've been away, so I went straight down to the basement to switch on the electricity. And that's when I found you in here!"

He looked annoyed, thought Poppy. But he didn't look nasty.

"Zach has been cleaning up your house," said Poppy. "Look in the kitchen."

Mr. Faltermeyer strode into the kitchen. "It does look much cleaner than I expected," he admitted. "But that doesn't make it right!"

Poppy thought hard. "Mr. Faltermeyer, we live next door. My name's Poppy, and this is my brother Sam. And this is KC, my best friend."

"Hi," said Sam and KC nervously.

"A few days ago, we saw a light on in your attic," Poppy continued, "and we decided to investigate." She started to tell Mr. Faltermeyer all about the mystery, but he stopped her.

"I think we need to sit down for this," he said. They all went into the front room. Mr. Faltermeyer sat on a chair and motioned Poppy to sit opposite him. Nobody else spoke as Poppy told the whole story. At first, Mr. Faltermeyer's face didn't move at all. It was impossible to tell what he was thinking.

When she got to the part about using the telescope to look into the attic, he frowned.

When she talked about Nicholas getting in trouble, he finally spoke. "Mrs. Linder," he said. "That's no surprise to me."

When she got to the part about Zach wanting to get away from his big family, he pursed his lips.

He looked at Poppy as she finished telling the story. She was sitting on the edge of her chair. She knew that if Mr. Faltermeyer wanted, he could complain to Poppy's parents. Poppy knew that she had done the right thing. Zach had to be rescued from the house. Her parents would believe her if she explained . . . wouldn't they?

"Poppy," said Mr. Faltermeyer, "I think there is something very important to do."

"Yes?" asked Poppy.

"We need to go over to Mrs. Linder's house," said Mr. Faltermeyer, "And have a talk with her!"

They all left the Dark House - except it wasn't the Dark House any more, Poppy realised. Lights were shining in every room now.

Zach, Poppy, KC and Sam crossed the street, with Mr. Faltermeyer in the lead. They passed a very grand old car parked outside.

"That must be Mr. Faltermeyer's car," said KC quietly. "Mrs. Linder said he drove one like that."

"What's he going to do?" whispered Sam.

"I don't know," said Poppy. "I really don't know."

Mrs. Linder opened the door. She had a phone in her hand. "Who is it now -" she started to say, and then saw Mr Faltermeyer. Her jaw dropped. She couldn't say anything. "It's you!" she said eventually.

"May we come in?" said Mr. Faltermeyer, pleasantly.

"Poppy, is that you?" A voice came from inside Mrs. Linder's house. "She's calling my mum and dad!"

"Nicholas!" Poppy called.

Soon, they were all inside. Nicholas was red-eyed. Mrs. Linder looked at Mr Faltermeyer. Poppy, KC and Sam tried to make themselves look as small as possible. Were the two grown ups about to join forces against them?

"Well, well," said Mr. Faltermeyer. "I found this boy in my house. These children," he said, pointing to Poppy, KC and Sam, "went in to save him when he got trapped in the attic."

Mrs. Linder scowled at Nicholas. "No. It was

this boy. I was about to call his parents, so they could punish him."

Mr. Faltermeyer looked at her strangely. "You were wrong, Mrs. Linder. And I hear you've been spreading rumours about me again."

Mrs. Linderman looked guilty. "I, um -"

"I think you owe this boy an apology," said Mr. Faltermeyer.

Mrs. Linder looked at Nicholas. Then she looked back at Mr. Faltermeyer with her beady eyes. Finally, she seemed to give in. "Oh, very well. I'm sorry, Nicholas," she said. "I suppose I was wrong about you."

"And?" asked Mr. Faltermeyer.

"And I'm sure you're a very nice boy. I'm sorry I doubted you, Poppy," finished Mrs. Linder. She looked a little bit ashamed, Poppy thought.

Nicholas looked at her. He didn't know what to say. But he was beginning to feel happier and started to smile.

"If these children hadn't worked so hard to find out what was going on in my house," said Mr. Faltermeyer, "then Nicholas would have been

punished for something he didn't do."

"But what about this child here?" said Mrs. Linder, pointing at Zach. "He's the real villain."

"Oh, Zach? I know Zach," said Mr. Faltermeyer casually. "I let him come in my house to clean it up."

"What?" said Mrs. Linder. Zach looked just as surprised as Mrs. Linder. "Well," said Mrs Linder, reluctantly. "In that case, I suppose I'd better . . . forget all about it. Hmph."

"And?" said Mr. Faltermeyer.

"And not poke my nose into other people's business, even if they do drive ridiculous, loud old cars," said Mrs. Linder.

"And now, we have to go!" Mr. Faltermeyer said, looking pleased with himself. He went out, followed by Nicholas, Zach, and the three friends. They crossed the street, and Mr. Faltermeyer looked at them.

"Thanks for saying that," said Zach, sheepishly. "You know, about me cleaning your house."

"That's all right, Zach," said Mr. Faltermeyer. "Mrs. Linder and I had an argument, years ago. Since then, she tells people that I was mean and grumpy. But I'm not. I can't wait to settle back into my house and get my garden looking good again.

"Now," he said to Zach, "I think you'd better go home and tell your parents where you've been. Maybe they'll teach you not to go into other people's houses!" But he didn't really look very stern.

Poppy thought he was actually happy to have made Mrs. Linder apologise. Zach ran off gratefully, calling good-bye.

"Goodnight to you, too," said Mr. Faltermeyer, turning to Poppy, KC and Sam. "You three are very brave. If I ever have a mystery that needs solving, I'll come to you!" He smiled, and went back inside his house; the house that wasn't the Dark House any more.

"I like Mr. Faltermeyer," said Poppy. "I hope we can help him out some time."

Nicholas gave all three friends a hug. "Wow!" he said. "You solved the mystery, and saved me, too. But how did you do it? What happened inside that house?"

"Come inside and have some biscuits, and we'll tell you," said Poppy. "It's a long story!"

Three Together

If you've enjoyed meeting Poppy,
KC and Sam, you can try one of these
other exciting books in the
Three Together series.